Grandpa's *Fishin'* Friend

Written by

Grandma Janet Mary™

A Gift from
Be the Star You Are®! Non Profit
PO Box 376
Moraga, Ca. 94556
877-944-STAR
www.bethestaryouare.org

Illustrated by

Craig Pennington

3rd book in the Grandma Janet Mary™ Series
My Grandma and Me *Publishers*

Acknowledgments

It doesn't seem possible that this dream, The Grandma Janet Mary™ Series, is already into its third book.
Countless hours of unpaid, dedicated work and a heartfelt commitment from a loyal, devoted family has made it all possible.

And so,
a special thanks to:

my daughters, Emily, my finance manager, and Sarah, my publicist, for their enthusiasm and unrelenting faith;
my husband, Mike, the man behind the scenes, in charge of shipping and inventory, and overall supervisor of a hundred other jobs;
my sons, daughters-in-law and sons-in law for their willingness to answer any and all calls when needed;
Natalie Pennington for her quiet strength and artistic talent;
Nicole Koenigsknecht, my niece, for her very special contribution to this book.

First Edition
Printed and bound in Canada
Friesen's of Altona, Manitoba

Library of Congress Cataloging-in-Publication Data on File

ISBN 0-9742732-2-8
LCCN 2004195767

Dedicated to

fishin' Grandpas everywhere,
those still with us
and those
whose memory we cherish.

To grandchildren of all ages,

All life is a miracle:
plants, earth, sky
and
fish that swim in water.

So,
take time to notice.
Take time to enjoy the miracles of life
with someone you cherish,
someone like your grandfather.

In that way,
you will come to know
the greatest miracle of all,
love given and love received.

With love,
Grandma Janet Mary™

There is no place I'd rather be . . .

. . . than sitting in this
boat,

together with
my grandpa now,

the two of us
afloat,

drifting. . .

. . . on this peaceful
lake.

It's here we both
are wishin'

that we would catch
some big ole' bass

as we sit here
a fishin'.

To those of you who love to fish,
I'm sure you would agree
that there is something sacred
'bout the lake and open sea.

And Grandpa says that God made fish
so guys like him could spend
an afternoon with someone who
becomes a fishin' friend.

My Grandpa smiles when thinking back
then says, "I know this gal.
She stole my heart. Your Grandma is
a darlin' fishin' pal.

And she can still catch any fish
with her amazing smile.
Your mom, she too, will fish with me.
She's good. She's got some style.

And these two ladies that I love
as fishin' friends, they're great.
But now it's you who has become
my favorite fishin' mate."

I listen
though I've heard
my Grandpa
say all this before.
And then,

I know just what
he'll do.
He points
up to the shore.

"Just north
of that there bend,"
he says,
"that's where they are,
I'd guess."

I bait my hook
like I was taught.
The worm guts
make a mess.

But,

Grandpa, he and I
don't care.
Our hands get clean
enough,

'cause we just use our fishin' pants
to wipe away gut stuff.

Then strong, old hands on weathered oars,
they slowly guide and lead.

He takes his time. He's in no rush,
one slow yet steady speed

now takes us north toward the bend
right to our fishin' site.

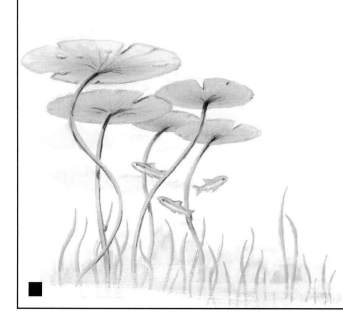

He drops the anchor. Grandpa winks.
It's here the fish will bite.

And how he knows, I'm not quite sure
but he sure knows a lot

about the fish that seem to swim
right to our fishin' spot.

Our lines are cast.
We sit and wait.
I stare at my
red bobber,

for I have learned
a fish can be
a thief with gills,
a robber.

He'll tease you,
nibble at your bait
then
when you look away,

he'll steal your worm
or leach or grub
and so
I vow this day,

to watch my bobber.
Stay Alert!
'cause there is quite
a catch

swimming
in this lake somewhere,
this fish I'd love
to snatch.

My Grandpa caught this special fish
last year when I was ten.
It was the biggest largemouth bass.
He reeled him in but then,

that bass slipped right through Grandpa's hands.
We gave that fish a name.
We call him Albert Einstein
'cause he's smart. He knows our game.

And when I think about that fish
I think of Grandpa too.
For he has taught me through the years,
one fact he says is true

that sometimes all it takes is luck,
this luck my Grandpa knows
is often found, it can be felt
in worn out fishin' clothes.

He sits there in his faded jeans.
The knees are slightly torn.
His shoes, he says he bought them
on the day that I was born.

"So,
that makes them real special shoes,"
my Grandpa says, "You see,
it is the stains and worn out soles
that bring good luck to me."

He always wears the same old shirt.
It's faded brown to tan
and on the front this smiling fish
says,
"Catch me if you can."

I love his faded pants and shirt.
His shoes are cool. They're neat.
But . . .

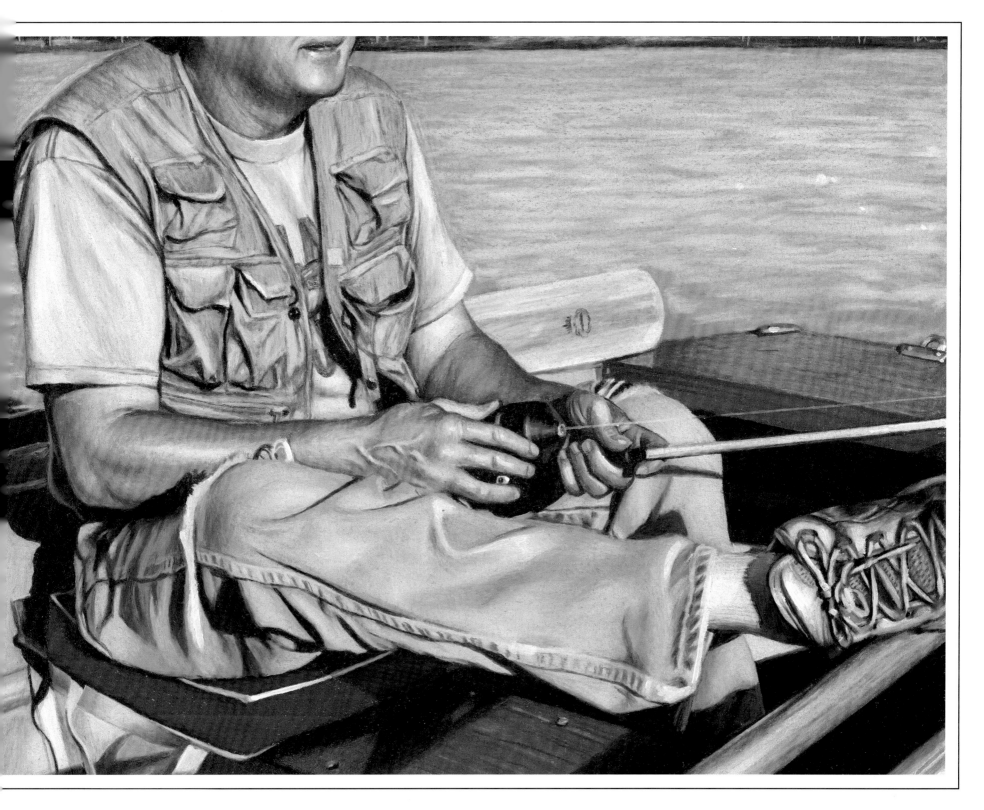

. . . it's my Grandpa's fishin' hat
that is so very sweet.
For dangling on his hat are lures
hooked just above the brim,

the ones that my Great-Granddad used,
and it was said of him,

that when he fished he always caught
the biggest bass and pike
and he believed it was his hat
that got the fish to strike.
So . . .

. . . I,
like Grandpa, have a hat
with lures that dangle too.

And Grandpa says,

"Our lures belonged
to your Great-Granddad
who . . .

. . . will be with us if we believe
his spirit never
dies.

And maybe

he will help us find where
Albert Einstein
lies."

And as I think about that fish
I feel a little jerk.
I look to see the bobber's gone.
It's time to get to work.

And so,
I pull and reel him in
the way that I've been taught.

But,
Darn it! It's not Einstein!
It's a bluegill that I've caught.

We fish the afternoon away.
We catch enough to eat.
But in my heart there's just one fish
that I would love to meet.

I stare into the water.

He's down there.

He's a thinker.

If only he would
swallow up

my hook, my line
and sinker.

We take a break
and lay on back
in Grandpa's little
boat.

The sun feels good.
It's warm enough
to fish without a coat.

For it's
a perfect summer day
and
life is really good.

The master angler
smiles and says,
"I do wish
that I could

spend every afternoon
with you.
It's been a lot of fun.

But,
now it's time
to row on in.
The day is almost done."

I touch the lures hooked to my hat
then beg, "Just one more time,
one final chance to try and catch
our fish we call Einstein."

He smiles then says, "Just one more time.
Cast out near all those weeds.
It could be that he's in there now
swimming while he feeds."

I do just like my Grandpa says.
I jig my heart away.
And just as I'm about to stop
and call it quits today,

I feel a sudden jerk.
My line, is reeling 'cross the lake,
The pull is strong. I scream,

"OH NO!
MY POLE'S ABOUT TO BREAK !

Please help me, Grandpa, reel him in."
But Grandpa says, "Stay calm.
This fish is yours. I'll coach you through.
You're strong just like your mom.

So listen now, just give him slack.
Be patient. We can wait,
'cause you have hooked him.
There's no doubt.
He really took the bait."

I listen to my Grandpa
as he whispers in my ear.
I pull and give and reel some more
until the fish is near.

And then,
at last I haul him up.
My Grandpa gets the net.

HE IS . . .

. . . the **BIGGEST** largemouth bass.

IT'S EINSTEIN!
I would bet!

I'm so excited as I stare
at this amazing fish.
And I am glad I caught him now.
I'm glad I got my wish.
But . . .

. . . as I sit here looking
at this fish we call Einstein.

It doesn't seem like it'd be right
to keep a fish so fine.

I look at Grandpa's face.
I see the same look in his eye.
I then recall last summer

and
I think I now know why,

my Grandpa never got upset
when Einstein did somehow
slip back into the lake like he's . . .

. . . about to do right now.
My mind is clear. I then announce,

"OUR EINSTEIN SHOULD GO FREE!"

For I can hear Great-Granddad's voice,
I think he's telling me . . .

. . . to put the old fish back
for there will be another day

to wear our hats with his old lures
and fish the day away.

My Grandpa nods
his head
and then together
we release

this great old fish
that Grandpa says
creates a sense
of peace.

"Who knows," he says.
"come spring or when
we ice fish in
December,

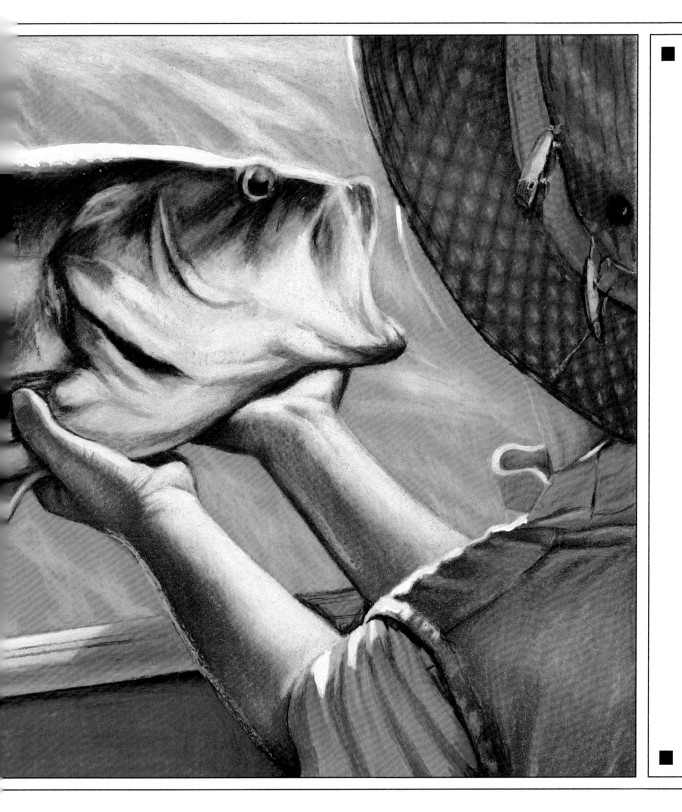

we just might hook
that fish again.
These times
you will remember.

And as you grow and
live your life,
think back on this
old fish.

Then share this story
with your kids.
Share a day like this."

I think about
the day we've had.
This time I won't forget.

And as we sit
and watch the sun
as it begins to set,

I smile because
of all the places
on this earth to see,

there is no spot
in this whole world
where I would rather be

than sitting here
with Grandpa thinkin'
'bout this special day,

the fun, the lessons
taught and learned,
the fish that slipped away.

And these new mem'ries
I will keep
and hold inside my heart,

so that one day
when I grow old
he still will be a part

of who I am
and who will be,
I'm thankful
I could spend . . .

. . . this perfect summer afternoon
with my best fishin' friend.

How to Catch a Largemouth Bass

Fishing terms and equipment

1. Master Angler...................... Someone who has fished many years, has learned patience, knows the mind of a fish and loves the quiet of the lake.
2. Jigging............................... Jerking the pole in an upward and downward motion. Jigging gets the fish interested.
3. Bait................................... Snack food for the fish. Fish love to eat live bait, for example: night crawlers, leeches, frogs, grubs, minnows. Some fish like artificial bait like: hoolapoppers, spinner and rattler baits or rubber worms.
4. Hook, Line, and Sinker.......... Basic equipment you will need if you want a fish dinner.
5. Fishing license..................... Check with Grandpa or other fisherman who know about the rules in your state.
6. Tackle box.......................... Contains all kinds of cool stuff you will need for fishing.
7. Life jacket.......................... You want to be safe. We weren't made to live in the lake like the fish.
8. Lots of patience................... You may have to wait for the fish to start biting. Be patient. Relax. Enjoy the day with Grandpa or whomever else you are blessed to be with.
9. Respect.............................. For the lake and all life within it. Be sure to bring a can or bag for throw away things.

Suggested technique

1. Cast out your line with fishing bait secure.
2. Keep your eye on the bobber.
3. When bobber starts bobbing and you can feel a tug on your pole then jerk the rod to hook the fish and start reeling in.
4. If the fish is big and a fighter, you may have to give some line and then reel some more.
5. Listen to instructions from your Grandpa or special fishin' friend.
6. Have someone hold the net to land your fish.
7. Take a break around lunchtime or whenever you get hungry. Enjoy a bologna or ham sandwich with other goodies packed by you or your Grandma.
8. Be sure to listen to old stories told by Grandpa. Share your thoughts. Make a lasting memory.

Would highly recommend a camera so you have proof of the big one that might get away!